Bee

Written by Jo Windsor

Rigby

Look at the beetles.

Beetles are in
lots of places.

2

Beetles can be big.
Beetles can be little.

Look at the colors
beetles can be.

5

Beetles can eat:

wood

leaves

clothes

A beetle can fly.

Where are the
beetle's wings?

8

The beetle's wings are under here.

The beetle's wings are under here.

9

Look at the beetle's wings.

The wings have opened up.

wing

10

wing

Look at the beetle.

Now the beetle
can fly!

Index

Guide Notes

Title: Beetles

Stage: Early (2) – Yellow

Genre: Nonfiction

Approach: Guided Reading

Processes: Thinking Critically, Exploring Language, Processing Information

Written and Visual Focus: Photographs (static images), Captions, Labels, Index

Word Count: 59

THINKING CRITICALLY

(sample questions)
- What do you think this book is going to tell us?
- Look at the title and read it to the children.
- Ask the children what they know about beetles.
- Focus the children's attention on the index. Ask: "What are you going to find out about in this book?"
- If you want to find out about wings, on what page would you look?
- If you want to find out what beetles eat, on what page would you look?
- What sort of places do you think you might find beetles in?
- What do you think is different about the way a beetle flies and the way a bird flies?

EXPLORING LANGUAGE

Terminology
Title, cover, photographs, author, photographers

Vocabulary
Interest words: beetles, colors, wood, leaves, clothes, wings
High-frequency word: be
Positional words: under, in

Print Conventions
Capital letter for sentence beginnings, periods, question mark, exclamation mark, colon